Really, Cher?

A Story with a Dog in It

Julian M. Coleman

Julian Coleman, Copyright 2015

ALL RIGHTS RESERVED

ISBN: 0990893952

To Erik for his undying support, and to my beloved Mina.

Table of Contents

Prologue

My name is Joy Bradford. I'm a rotund mom who has had some joyless years in my life, but I'm not complaining. There's been more happiness than pain. I don't smoke, I don't gamble, and except for chocolate, which is my *drug* of choice, I don't do drugs. I'm okay with my addiction.

Large women don't eat any chocolate on television. Actually, large women are invisible in pop culture. You don't believe me? Take a look at the commercials. We don't exist to sell many "attractive" things. It's like we don't have money. Even the dating websites don't show us. I believe that weight diversity is virtually nonexistent.

But this story isn't about my pounds. It is about my relationship with my pooch.

I prefer male dogs. Yes, I do, and I'm proud to acknowledge that ... most of the time.

There is that level of testosterone I'm used to dealing with in a male canine persona. They have traits like aggressiveness, attitude, and cleverness in achieving an end despite the consequences. Yes, I'm still talking about canines.

Here's my example: If confronted with a juicy steak on a kitchen table, a male dog may consider being "good" but usually there's no dilemma, no crisis of conscience. From his perspective, if the chef of a scrumptious grilled meat was stupid enough to leave the room, well then, damn the risks and full meat ahead. Bone appétit. Chomp, chomp.

A female dog like Cherie—or Cher, as she is lovingly referred to by other family members (to me she is just plain Bee-itch), is often calculating but also very, very patient. No stealing the chomps from her. She's better at looking pitiful, thus loading up a pile of "poor-starving-me" like a plateful of pasta until I feel compelled to give her half my meal. She has never absconded with any food. Ever.

It is episodes like I just described that force me to believe that males are riskier while females are calculating. I'm still talking about canines.

I've suffered Cher for years. We've been together from spinsterhood to grandchild to marriage. She loves my husband, and daughter. She adores my granddaughter. But she hates me. Maybe hate is too strong a word? Maybe it's jealousy or just plain old contempt? Read and judge.

These are her tales (or my story about a roguish she-dog with a diva complex).

Chapter 1:
Sunny-Girl? Are you serious?

I can't tell the Cher tale without first enlightening you about Mario. Their tales, not their tails, are entwined.

We adopted Mario first. He was this sucker's compromise.

My saga begins with my daughter, Zane. She is, and has always been, supersmart. She used to make excellent grades in school seemingly without any mental exertion. She used to piece together Lego bricks before she could talk. By the time she was in kindergarten, her Lego designs had functionality. There were to be no silly dolls for Zane. She was destined to be an engineer.

One day my very bright 6-year-old daughter asked for a sibling. As a single parent with zero dating choices, much less falling in love and getting married, I decided that in vitro, adoption, and cloning weren't options. So how was giving my one and only a sibling going to happen?

By chance, 101 Dalmatians had hit the theaters. We'd seen the movie, and I saw an opportunity for a compromise. "What about a Dalmatian?"

Zane focused those huge brown eyes on me. She smiled deviously and said, "Okay." She had agreed too easily and too soon after we had seen the movie. I suspected then that I had been duped, so there was no need to congratulate myself on being clever.

Merriam-Webster's Dictionary: sucker (n) – a person who is easily tricked.

Chapter 1: Sunny-Girl? Are you serious?

We adopted Mario from a breeder. He didn't have any dots on his face except for thin rings around his eyes that looked too much like mascara. He was beautiful. Zane had named him after her favorite video game character. Despite rows of sharp teeth, his smile was beguiling.

Initially, he had a pink nose, a flaw that made him a Dudley. I thought the pink nose also made him interesting, so I was disappointed when his pink nose turned black.

Mario's brown eyes were so alluring that I didn't mind tossing him part of my dinner. But if I decided not to supplement his dinner with my own, well he had his remedy. He happily toppled the kitchen trashcan over in the wee morning hours and helped himself to juicy discards. So yes, Mario was a bit of a spoiled canine. He ruled our household for twelve glorious years.

Mario never seemed to age. He had grace and poise, and he remained spry even as he started aging into his double digits. Sadly, after twelve years his health declined suddenly at the same time my life took a downturn.

Yes, my life took a hard downturn. This is my polite way of saying that the pilings that supported my existence rotted all at once. I did a slip-slide into hell with only my dignity super-gluing my heart together.

First, I was downsized, don't you hate that word, out of a glamorous job. I used to crisscross the country meeting customers, and giving presentations. I loved my supervisor. My coworkers were like family. I wasn't a barracuda in the corporate fishbowl. I didn't need power, or money to feel whole. I was in my dream job. I just wanted to stay there until I retired.

Profits are what drive corporations and my company had been on the losing end of a merger. In the newly merged company, my dream job disappeared despite pre-merger assurances. My travel days ended which meant there were no more stays in luxurious hotels; no more *per diems* spent on pricey meals or driving expensive rental cars. Worse than that, I was forced to take a lower position and a hefty pay cut. So, what was worse than the loss of pay and prestige? How about those consolatory pats on the back, and well-meaning tsk-tsks, from folks who seemed to enjoy reminding me, here it comes, that *at least I still had a job.*

During that same downturn, Carla, a dear friend, who bullheadedly insisted on smoking despite a lung cancer scare, died. No one had ever loved me and hated me with the same intensity as Carla. She had been the seasoning salt to my existence. When she'd died, my world became bland ... and colorless.

She had always been rowdy, bawdy, and just plain fun. She had an infectious, almost dirty laugh, and enormous breasts which she enjoyed squeezing at the most inappropriate time, namely around men she found attractive.

Carla had been in remission so I'd coaxed myself into some sort of self-serving denial. I wanted to believe that she would survive for years, which left me emotionally unprepared when she passed away. To this day, I still dream about her.

I needed Mario. Months earlier, before he became sickly, we had a family *discussion*. We had just suffered another tsunami of teen-angst drama from Zane. Frankly, Mario and I had decided that we wanted the girl gone. The girl even stopped having a name. We had reduced her to a caricature although the girl was by now officially a woman.

We saw that in the girl, logic and hormonal angst were mutually exclusive. It was a great day in the land of singlehood when I could finally load up the van with her belongings and shuttle her off to college ... in another state.

But when I came home, it was to some horrible news. Mario, who had been kenneled at the vet's office, had suffered a setback. His health had taken a downturn.

My veterinarian, an olive-skinned hunk who I secretly called Dr. Gorgeous, had been talking. I remember that his words seem to come to me from another dimension. I thought I heard Dr. Gorgeous telling me that Mario wasn't just sick; he was terminal. Dr. Gorgeous had said something about the tumor's location made it inoperable. I kept hearing the word, "suffering."

Suffering and Mario? I couldn't connect the two.

I tried to embrace the reality. Mario had been doped up against his pain for some time, but again I had been delusional. Now I realized that we wouldn't get the chance to celebrate our liberation from the girl. I was going to be alone. If I loved him then I had to let him go.

I started to have flashbacks in the veterinarian's office.

I remembered when Zane had picked out Mario from the litter and how the breeder had gently suggested, "You don't want that one." Of course, with that endorsement, Zane had picked him up and put him in the car. The breeder had been right—Mario had been a handful of polka-dotted testosterone.

I also remembered the time Mario had duped me into blaming Zane for eating most of the chicken. It was easy for him to do since Zane and I didn't eat dinner together. When faced with a near-empty plate, I had just assumed that Zane's version of teen angst also included eating up all the chicken. During a blow-up, we realized Mario was the real chicken snatching culprit. No wonder he was always so attentive whenever I prepared his favorite meat.

I could still see him sitting patiently in the kitchen and watching me with almost laser beam-like attention. Baked or fried, I should've known when only the chicken disappeared.

Mario, my dear, greedy scoundrel.

I heard myself agree to euthanasia on the spot. Dr. Gorgeous was amazing those last few moments of Mario's life. We sat on the floor. Mario's head was in my lap. Dr. Gorgeous administered a tranquilizer before injecting Mario with the kill shot.

I tried in vain not to cry because I didn't want Mario to see me distressed. Mario thumped his tail one last time. Then he was gone. The light just left his eyes. I wept openly as I kissed the top of his head, and said goodbye.

My depression failed to lift and reached a peculiar bottom when one morning I stumbled through the living room to let Mario out. His demanding barks had awakened me from a disturbing nightmare. My hand was on the doorknob when I remembered that he was gone. His barking faded as would any smoky dream. With my hand still on the doorknob, I wept.

I survived, as I always do, by first crying my eyes out, then by counting my blessings. I was sad, broke, and alone. Life continued. I tried to be valiant. I tried to cope.

A few times I allowed myself to give in to bits of insanity only because it helped to coat over the hurt. So yes, occasionally I would open the back door and call out to Mario.

I knew that he was gone, but shouting out his name gave me some comfort. My neighbors may have been a bit disturbed since they knew he was gone. Some probably wondered if they were living next to a crazy woman.

I thought I was saved when, six months after Mario's death, Dr. Gorgeous' office called to tell me about a stray dog that needed a home. The receptionist said the staff was reluctant to send her to the local dog shelter because of the low odds of her surviving. Dr. Gorgeous had suggested me.

I agreed to take the stray unseen. It was a stupid move, but a new dog would ease me out of my loneliness. She would have a new home, and I would have a companion, but a female dog?

Merriam-Webster Dictionary: stupid (n) – slow of mind: obtuse

As I drove to the vet's office, I tested out cutesy girl names.

And then I met her.

The stray was a mutt that resembled a small German shepherd. She looked more wolfish than domesticated canine. Her coat was brindle, almost the same color as my skin, with irregular dark markings that looked like zigzag lines of tar. She had wolf ears that she rotated like antennas. The staff gushed about her cheerful personality. Clearly that persona had departed as soon as I had entered. We studied each other cautiously like opposing gunslingers facing off in a dusty western town.

She just seemed standoffish and sneaky to me. Maybe it was just me. Maybe I was emitting a vibe that was sloughing off like dandruff. But I saw what I saw. We were eying each other suspiciously.

The staff had field tested several corny names for her like Sunny-Girl. I smiled politely at them as I secretly scoped out the nearest exit.

Sunny-Girl had on a pink collar. She had been someone else's pet, but there were no identification tags on the collar. Dr. Gorgeous had estimated that she was possibly a year old.

Although to me she was aloof, I had already agreed to take her home. So, like everything else I saw this challenge as a blessing. They had even supplied her with shots and a microchip. Shucks, there was no getting rid of her now.

Sunny-Girl's tail drooped noticeably when her lead was handed over to me. I thought to myself: *Don't think it's just you, girly. I feel the same way.*

But I had a promise to keep. I also reminded myself that if I didn't take her then, her odds of survival at the dog pound were bleak. So, I smiled through clenched teeth.

Sunny-Girl—had to get rid of that name—climbed into my Subaru. She stared at me as she settled onto the backseat.

Chapter 1: Sunny-Girl? Are you serious?

I wish I could say the drive was uneventful, but it wasn't. What I did notice was that her royal highness wasn't interested in hanging her head out of the window like a typical male dog.

Mario used to insist that I crack the windows open. He would dash from side to side while slobbering on the windows. Riding was a treat. He loved the nostril banquet, and he knew who was driving, too.

I don't know when Cherie officially got her name. But it could've been when I was yelling at her to sit in the backseat and desist from trying to take the wheel.

She had a dog license. I had a driver's license. There is a big blanking difference!

We had scarcely left the parking lot when I had dog breath in my ear. I knew then that we were in trouble. Using the console as leverage, I saw that she was one leap away from taking the wheel. A nudge sent her to the back seat, but she sprang forward again just like a yo-yo.

It was obvious that she was excited by this new game. I realized then too that I had just acquired yet another dog with a sneaky smile.

My mom is renowned for her side-seat driving. She's great at suggesting better routes after it's too late to take them. However, mom has nothing on Cher's side-seat driving. Cher seemed to edge closer to the steering wheel after each nudge.

By the time we reached home, I behaved like one of those folks who drop to their knees and kiss the ground in gratitude after enduring a harrowing journey.

Seething, I opened the passenger door for her royal highness. She flopped out of the car without a trace of remorse or grace, and I led her into my fenced-in backyard. Once she was secure, I went back to the car to retrieve my purse. I opened the front passenger door and immediately saw that Cher was standing by my side. She looked as if she were ready to go on another ride. Maybe I hadn't secured the gate?

I led her, again, into the backyard. I latched the gate properly, and after double checking it, I went back to my car. I reached inside to get my purse, closed the door and sure enough, she was standing by my side.

What in the—?

The gate was still closed, but my chain-link fence was only three feet high. She was a jumper!

Now I understood how a well-fed dog with a pink collar, but no identification, had happened to get lost. To borrow a misquoted phrase: "Fairfax, I have a problem."

My modest home sat in the middle of an acre of land. It was backed up by woods. I'd never gone into those woods. A fox, snapping turtles, and snakes had all emerged from those woods. Their appearances were a clear "Do Not Enter" sign to me. I was lawful. I obeyed the sign. The jumper was an affront to my terms of agreement. If she jumped the fence, then who would go in there to get her? Me?

I ushered the flight-risk into my home, grabbed the phone and called up Dr. Gorgeous' office. Sunny-Girl, newly named Cher grinned up at me, or was she actually laughing, as I explained my dilemma. I hesitated to call it a game changer. Dr. Gorgeous seemed amused. Somehow, he missed the chilliness in my tone. He suggested electronic fencing. Ta-dah, problem solved! Click.

I fumed.

A dog that needed a home, and that wasn't going to cost me a cent, was now possibly going to cost me hundreds, if not thousands of dollars.

Just great!

Chapter 2:
Dingo is her Breed–o

Cher and I peacefully coexisted. We developed a routine that included me doing a lot of nagging, but very little touching. Mario had lived with me for more than a decade, so it was difficult reconciling *her* presence in *his* house. I still missed him. Sometimes it felt like betrayal whenever she nudged my heart.

I never expected her behavior to mirror his. Mario was obviously well-bred. I hate to put it that way, but clearly, he had breeding. He trotted through my home, which was also known as his doghouse, with his head held majestically. His tail wagged perpetually, and he was rarely unhappy. When he did something simple like lying down, he did it in a manner where he eased back, dropped his hind legs and slowly but elegantly unlocking his forelegs.

Perhaps he would yawn, yes, there were spots inside his mouth too, and then he would roll over and sleep. When it was time to eat, he was in the habit of eating a little bit and walking away. By morning, though, his bowl would be empty.

Cher, in contrast, seemed to have been dragged up from the gutter. There wasn't an elegant bone in her body. She was so greedy that I spent a great deal of time training her not to rush me when I filled her bowl.

She loved to eat. She gobbled noisily until her bowl was empty, and then she would spend the next minute licking it clean. After the disgusting sounds of her gobble-chomp serenade, I would be treated to her water-slurps until the water dish was nearly empty too.

When she was tired, Cher would just drop onto the ground without any measure of grace. She sounded like a tired old bag of bones that had been plopped down on the hardwood floor. The first time I had heard that strange sound I wondered where it had come from and if I could make it stop. When lying down, she had a habit of pointing her butt toward me. Sometimes when I called her from that position, she would strain to lift her head just so that I could see the look of contempt on her face. Or worse, she would just fart.

Hazmat, help me.

My real problem? She was smart. I mean she was scary smart, and it became clear that she thought that she was smarter than me. She understood some rudimentary commands such as sit, or eat—her favorite. But she was still leaping the fence higher than Santa's reindeer, and quite often too.

I was reluctant to get the electronic fence, not only because it would've crapped on my wee budget, but also because I personally couldn't train her through electric shocks. Yes, it was preferable to a dead dog, but there had to be a kinder way … ah yes, dog training.

What I had been reduced to was bribery and chaining up, which I was ashamed of using without abandon. In the mornings, I let her out into the backyard to do her business— why do we call it that? To be polite?—Then I would bribe her with a treat to get her greedy butt back inside the house.

My ploy worked most mornings, but every so often she would stand in front of the fence, always at the same spot, look over at me as if she were daring me to argue, and just leap for freedom. When I wasn't seething, I thought she looked quite graceful. Jumping was much nicer than giving me the middle finger. Maybe it was her way of doing just that?

So yes, there were mornings when I was running through my neighbors' yards in dew-soggy slippers, while clutching my robe. Naturally, such predawn dashes woke me up quicker than downing pints of black coffee.

One course of dog obedience training coming right up!

Cher's greed was a perfect fit for training. Each successfully accomplished task was rewarded with a treat. Naturally she adapted to her commands quickly. She was a hungry student who easily won an impromptu competition.

Really?

The training was a waste of money. In addition to keeping her in the yard, I had hoped the training would make walking Cher easier. Neither outcome happened. Walking Cher was a chore because she constantly pulled on her lead. She understood what "leave it," "come," "stay" all meant, but my very smart she-bitch wasn't having any of that command nonsense.

See Cher.

See Cher jump the fence.

See Cher run.

Television saved me, or to be accurate, a personable but firm television dog trainer saved me. He taught me that I had to assume the leader role. I started using his *free* techniques, and they worked.

I became Cher's drill sergeant. Now she had consequences for jumping. The jumps didn't completely stop but they dwindled. Plus, pleasant walks were easier to accomplish. There were consequences there too. Whenever she pulled on her lead or stopped during a walk to sniff the urine, I would snap her toward me with a jerk while forcing her head up and thus allowing her no wiggle room. It worked.

We frequently walked which also cut down, but didn't totally eliminate, her desire to jump. To help her burn energy without burning mine, I taught her how to fetch.

Begrudgingly, we bonded.

But what I couldn't understand was her muteness. Such a fierce looking dog never seemed to bark.

I had a philosophy. My dogs worked in my house. Their jobs included serving as burglar alarms. Teaching a dog to bark used to be easy, but I had given up on Cher. She would make a barking sound, sometimes, but that was not her mode of communication.

Mario used to bark to exit the house, bark to reenter, bark when the wind was too loud or plain just because he wanted to—Cher herded. She would move in front of me and try to guide me to the door, to her bowl, or anywhere else she wanted me to go. A little nudging was not uncommon. They had very different personalities.

Or did they?

It happened on a Saturday. I was cleaning the house. I was feeling low. I had applied for a job, but I had been edged out because of outright favoritism. A close friend of the selecting official had beaten me to the job, and yes, that applicant's qualifications were far less impressive than mine. Not that I had wanted the position, but I was eating through my savings just to pay the bills. My bank account was on life support. I needed a job to be on firmer financial ground.

I was thinking about this dilemma as I was vacuuming. That was when I saw Cher on television. Only it wasn't Cher. I had been looking at a family movie, and the dog looked exactly like mine—they were twins. How could my mutt have a twin in a movie? She was a mutt, wasn't she? I sought Cher who was sleeping in her bed, and asked, "What kind of dog are you?"

She lifted her head, looked at me as if I were disturbing her sleep, and plopped her head back down.

I parked in front of my computer and began searching for answers. My research didn't take long. I compared key features including the split down the middle of her forehead, the white paws, all four of them, the white that ran under her chin and down her underbelly—and her lack of voice ... um bark. A dingo? Are you kidding me? Did they give me a dingo?

Sometimes ignorance is truly bliss.

Did someone breed a wild dog and didn't account for the nature of that breed to be a little wild? Jumping a fence is nothing to a "breed" that can climb a tree.

Dingoes eat babies, don't they?

Chapter 3:
The Grandpuppy

I was surprised to find out that I was a grandmother.

Was it pleasant? Not at first.

Zane had detoured off the college road after one year. She did an encore show from her early teen angst years beginning with the "find herself tour" which she hoped was enough to explain why her back was velcroed to the couch.

I watched her potentially lucrative career in engineering fizzle out. I saw years of financial sacrifice for her private school education rendered meaningless, except that I was still paying for it. Couldn't she have at least graduated from college?

Cher gave me her usual head tilted, ears rotating, and wide-eyed stare as I absorbed this shock. I hated to admit that Cher seemed to understand even when my daughter didn't. Cher consoled me when Zane further squandered her potential to work at a video store.

My colorful advice had all the nuances of perpetual nagging, so she moved in with her boyfriend. I didn't stop there, but I should've. Zane withered under my blistering advice and quite frankly she disappeared from my life. I wasn't told about Lillie's birth until my grandchild was a month old. I pretended my omission at such a pivotal moment in Zane's life didn't hurt. To this day, there is still a scar from that wound.

In my heart, Lillie redeemed my daughter, somewhat. I couldn't stay angry when Lillie was such a beautiful joy. As my only grandchild, it was my right to spoil her crazy.

Plus, I believed her parents were too lax.

Lillie didn't recognize behaviors like going to bed at a proper time. She scoffed at discipline, and thought the word "no" was a foreign language. It wasn't her fault that she was a brat, but she certainly did seem to enjoy being mischievous.

It didn't help that she was beautiful, either. She had a cherub's face, full cheeks ripe for the pinching, thick black hair, and creamy tawny brown skin. The only thing missing from that package was a pair of angelic wings—or little demonic horns.

To me, it seemed that smart dogs, and smarter babies, learned early the benefits of batting long eyelashes to get their ways.

In the contest between the two divas, poor Cher didn't stand a chance. Oddly, not that she minded. She gave Lillie full rein to brutalize her. I actually think it was love.

Cher had been spayed before I adopted her, so her days were filled with sleeping, walking, or eating. She didn't jump the fence quite as often because she knew that she would get into trouble, or more likely, she was getting too fat to leap the fence even with a running start.

I think Cher saw Lillie as her puppy. I tried to keep Lillie, who was more dangerous when she was mobile, from tugging on Cher—a tail, or an ear, it didn't matter.

Cher was a dingo, and everyone knew "dingoes ate babies." Except that Cher was as wild as a hangnail. I mean all our wars involved wills, but no teeth or growls. Her sole desire was to outsmart me as often as possible.

But with Lillie, she melted like ice cream under hot chocolate sauce. Her eyes would go round and soft whenever Lillie was near. And one of Lillie's first words was, "Cher."

Cher was redeemed by me whenever Lillie looked at her with the kind of love I could only dream of getting from her. Every time I babysat, and it was just the three of us, one of us didn't matter. Lillie played with her Cher, cuddled her Cher, pulled, poked, and prodded her Cher.

There was no dead baby, only a loved baby.

When Lillie became verbal, I heard her announce, "I love you," to Cher while she gave her a hug. I was invisible, and I couldn't have been happier.

There was a caveat to all this love.

Cher could only take so much. When Lillie's affections became too intense, Cher would often hide near me, her enemy, for protection. I could always tell too when she had had enough by the way her ears rotated as if she was sending out an SOS. I would give her cover while reminding her that she owed me.

Since Cher couldn't have puppies, I made up for this deficiency by purchasing her toys. She loved the ones that squeaked whenever she bit into them. Yes, she loved those the most. Cher couldn't nip at Lillie, but she would seize her toys, her babies as I called them, and rip them apart. She seemed to take satisfaction in yanking out the stuffing, and the squeaker, and then scattering the appendages thither. She would still care for the main body, which seemed bizarre, as if it were an intact baby.

Lillie has grown older. She's smart, and I'm not saying that just because I'm her grandmother. She's also a bit of a bully. We're all working on that. Cher still loves her, and Lillie is a lot more respectful. She still announces first and foremost that she loves Cher. I always get second billing, if I get any billing at all.

Now I know better. When Lillie comes over, I'd better hide the babies.

Chapter 4:
Him

Cher comforted me during one of my bleakest periods.

What did Friedrich Nietzsche say? *That which does not kill us makes us stronger*? I'm not so sure that's true. A series of losses and financial blows didn't kill me, but they made me weaker instead of stronger. Even a stoic alien whose creed was not to express any emotion would've wept under my circumstances.

I had to survive. I needed to concentrate on my financial wellbeing. I had grasped the only job offered, a paraprofessional job. At once I was grappling with the loss of pay and prestige. I went from flying to Philly, Laguna Nigel, or Chicago where I evaluated processes and programs to relying on my word processing skills and filing. My ego was bruised.

Girl, you're lucky to still have a job.

I smiled and thought, *bite me*, at the same time.

I was just so tired of hearing that chorus from the "glad I'm-not-you refrain." It was as grating as a needle stuck in the groove of a crackling 45 record. Acquaintances were well-meaning, but their words stung.

Yes, I was lucky to have a job, some type of income, but things were bad, and I wanted my old life back. I sent out résumés like a crazy person. The saying, "it's all about the Benjamins," sadly was true in my case. I needed those hundred-dollar bills to boost my income and I couldn't afford to be picky. Or that was my thought.

I was so wrong.

I had a solid work background, a Bachelor of Science degree, and a glowing evaluation, but I was experienced—meaning older—and not everyone saw experience as a benefit. Although it seemed longer than it was, I snagged an interview with an up-and-coming department. I sailed through the interview without sweating buckets. Still, I was surprised when I was selected. The new job not only restored my sense of self-worth, but also filled my pockets with more money than I had made previously in my dream job.

But good things don't happen to me.

The ensuing chaos was my fault. I had interviewed for a job without interviewing my interviewers. In simpler words, I had unknowingly stepped waist deep in it.

The executive was nice enough. She was a DC hotshot, a new honcho with loads of big ideas. It was her second-in-command, her right-hand man ... uh, woman, who had raised an inconsequential question, or in retrospect, a subtle protest against my selection during my interview. She had questioned my lack of knowledge about a software application. It was a minor point that should've raised a red flag to me, but since the executive glossed over the question, I placed no significance on it, or her.

I hadn't missed that exchange; I had ignored it. I had only wanted to wow the executive with my brilliance and personality that I had failed to pay attention to the other. The first-in-command wanted me. Her second-in-command had earmarked the position for a friend of hers; at least that was what I had later found out.

Chapter 4: Him

Guess who was tasked with training me for my new position?

Yes, she was my coach, and she drove my excursion bus straight into hell. Since Miss Right-Hand was the gateway to the executive that meant that everyone was nice to her, and that meant she ruled by proxy. I learned quickly to hide behind false smiles as I tried to blend into the landscape.

Honestly, I'm not good at politics but I do excel in getting the job done. I would learn that the work didn't matter. Neither organizational goals nor corporate missions were important as Miss Right-Hand's true narcissistic face revealed itself.

Several times during my career, I had found myself targeted by nasty management crosshairs. This time, I was financially and emotionally unequipped to deal with the drama that played out around, and because of, me. Plus, I was too new on the job to have formed any alliances.

Merriam-Webster Dictionary: screwed (v) - treated so as to bring about injury or loss (as to a person's reputation).

Although I was depressed, and that may have colored my perspective, I could still see that my career was being sabotaged. The taut body languages and whispers were all around me. Folks avoided me or wouldn't return my phone calls. Well-meaning others would state, casually and off the record, "You'd better watch your back."

Invitations to pivotal meetings failed to make it to my inbox. My good ideas, the few that I had, were confiscated, but the bad ones were all mine alone. The executive, my one true ally, started to send direct instructions through Miss Right-Hand. Suddenly there was a need to reduce my pay? Ouch!

For a time, I mindlessly indulged in victim cake coated with woe-is-me icing served with a scoop of why-did-I-deserve-this ice cream. Miss Right-Hand was actively swapping me out for the preferred employee, her friend.

I had two choices. I could try to keep doing what I was doing which only seemed to help my exodus to unemployment, or I could beef up my résumé by going back to school and getting my master's degree.

I hated option two. But it was the only option I had to actively save my career. My conversations with Miss Right-Hand were becoming more condescending, even demeaning. Others, I noticed, were talking down to me too, if they bothered to speak at all.

I certainly don't believe that a diploma indicates intelligence, but I was desperate, again. Yes, my beefed-up résumé would make me more marketable. Also, that piece of paper would take the bite out of rumors that I was too stupid to put toilet paper in my hand before I wiped my behind.

Even Cher, my nemesis, seemed to intuit my dilemma and by her demeanor deemed me as pathetic. If she offered any sympathy, it was only because she wondered if I would be able to afford her food. I wouldn't have been surprised if she jumped the fence again just so that she could find a new home. After all, her self-serving strategy had worked on me.

Now she was used to a certain lifestyle, and she was going to keep it. She obviously loved being a kept pooch. Sleep outside? Not unless she wanted to nap on the deck. Sleep on the floor? Maybe, but the futon was full of cushions. Tasty treats and snacks? Keep them coming.

Although leaping to freedom may now seem like a memory, Cher still received her morning treats. If I was late providing her treats, well, that was corrected with a nudge and a whine. After all, we must keep protocols in place.

Did I mention that she was getting fat?

Long walks, which she insisted on even when I was dog tired, pun intended, plus episodes of fetch, did nothing to impede her girth. She wasn't obese, but she was chunky. I didn't know that pooches could have double chins.

I have to admit that there were times when she was like therapy. At the end of a crapfest day, I would deflate on the couch, prop my feet up on the table, and drown my sorrows in too much pasta and glasses of red wine. Cher would place her head in my lap and commiserate. Even though life had gotten harder, I was never alone with Cher by my side. Sometimes she got extra treats. Sometimes I did too. But I'm rambling.

I enrolled in one of those universities that had a satellite campus for working adults. The programs were accelerated, which meant I was giving up all my free time. Going back to school was like sucking down a spoonful of bitter medicine. I tried to drink it down fast, and hoped that I wouldn't taste a thing.

I hated working stress-filled long hours, and then end the day sitting in a classroom for an additional four hours, even if it was once a week. The MBA program had imposing courses with titles like Operations Management, Business Research Methods, and Financial Accounting, but the mountains of homework redirected my energy. I had a blade buried in my posterior, but the pain was blunted by my new purpose.

The program consisted of workgroups or teams. The teams were typically comprised of five or more members, but my team was unusual because it was so small. There were only three of us. We parceled the research and presentation burdens evenly amongst ourselves. Our grades were exceptional because we were close and innovative. Conflicts rarely happened ... I mean, God knew that I had enough conflicts on the job.

Overall my classmates and teammates were nice. The class loved to party. They got together often, and any pseudo-reason did just fine, thank you. I was in too much agony to celebrate anything. I would hear about the parties, shrug my shoulders and plod on in my eternal cycle of work, school, and team meetings. Hit repeat.

I met *him* at school.

He was on a different team. We rarely spoke. I was too focused on my precarious balance of straddling employment versus unemployment to notice a man. Still, I noticed that Eddie was the kind of person who bought goodies to share each time we moved from one arduous course to another. He would hand out muffins or cookies before the new professor had a chance to dampen our spirits with a litany of demands, i.e., syllabus. Eddie's goodies engaged the class in celebrating another milestone.

Our paths merged when the nicest guy in the class turned his chivalry on me. Finances and personal obligations broke up my original team. I went from a three-member team to solo. There was no solo "team" in the MBA program.

Why on earth did I have the worst luck?

A duo decided to help me out by leaving their team and joining me. Although I was still the third leg of another trio, the energy was not the same. Yes, our work was exemplary, but that trusting dynamic to lean on each other was absent. I didn't trust them. I also sensed that I was being discussed behind my back.

Since I was "going through" an employment tragedy at work, I decided not to rely on my instincts. I cajoled myself into thinking that I was paranoid. Not everyone was out to get me. I wasn't important. In fact, the leadership course ended very well, and we celebrated our *As*.

At the start of the new course, the incoming professor wanted to identify the teams. It was at that moment, the moment of team announcement, that I discovered those two scoundrels had ditched me, and I was solo, again. I felt as if everyone was staring at me. Why couldn't I keep a team together? Was I a jinx? I was starting to wonder that myself.

It was humiliating. Those two hadn't demonstrated one iota of courtesy. They had jettisoned me without a heads-up. In that stillness, I felt the eyes of every classmate on me, except those two, and the sympathetic grimace of the new professor. I burned with embarrassment. Then, I heard a voice say, "You can join our team, Joy."

Eddie smiled at me. My heart pranced.

I hadn't set out to be a damsel in distress. I was quite proud that I had achieved my accomplishments based on my sweat. But when Eddie, who hadn't checked with his teammates, pointed to a vacant seat near his, I joined the new and larger group.

The new team's energy was down-to-earth. Or was that just my attraction to Eddie.

He was a soldier, a true *green* boy scout of Asian and Italian descent. Bespectacled and with a receding hairline, he was also quite hot. We started dating, although we kept our relationship mum. My blossoming romance kept my work life turmoil from turning me into jelly.

Plus, Cher had someone new to sniff.

I didn't mind sharing my gallant soldier with my brindle diva. In little time, it was noticeable that Cher loved Eddie too. She could be stingy with her affections, but never with him.

Somehow, I ended up being the outsider looking in. Her tail wagged harder when she was near him. She jumped on the couch and placed her head in his lap. It was obvious to *me* that I had no place in her new relationship.

What in the hell happened to the loving pooch who had offered me sympathy, if only to help me keep her food bowl filled? Did she let a man come between us?

Really, Cher?

She would stop to see if Eddie needed her first whenever I called. She whined incessantly whenever he left the house. I never heard a peep when I left, but I suspected she celebrated my departures by standing up on her hind legs and performing a Scottish jig. I wondered if she could, would she say, "Good riddance, and don't forget to pick up some more treats!"

By this time, Cher and I had tolerated each other for a few years. She was my best friend. She was granddog to my spoiled granddaughter. And yet, she had tossed me over for a man just like any backstabbing guest on one of those skin-cringing daytime talk shows. Just wow.

Eddie had grown up around dogs. He came from a large family, but he had admitted that he never paid attention to his dogs. Well, his interactions must've been limited. Whenever I complained about Cher's conniving behavior, he would tsk-tsk my observations. Dogs didn't do those things.

Huh?

Okay. Well, what he didn't know was that with Cher school was in session, and he was about to get a different kind of education.

The first lesson occurred when I asked him why Cher, who was sitting by his side, insisted on keeping her paw over his hand. We were watching television when he saw this and moved his hand aside. Cher just as quickly dropped her paw over his hand again. It became a game until Eddie gave up and let her have her way with her paw atop his hand. He wondered if that look on Cher's face was intolerance. Maybe he was just projecting? I laughed.

He asked, "Why is she doing it?"

"Ownership."

"What?"

I said, "She's taking charge of you. She owns you."

As I shared earlier, Cher did a good imitation of barking, but mostly she was mute—sometimes for days. What she did well was to herd. She would glance back periodically to see if any adjustments were necessary. I have seen her block an entrance until I was headed for either the door, so that she could get her walk, or to her food dish so that she could—well, you know.

Eddie, the friendly soldier, was oblivious to her tacit requests. He thought taking Cher for daily walks was his idea.

He reminded me of myself when I had enrolled Cher in that expensive dog obedience class. She was, without exception, the smartest dog in the room, but at the end of her dog obedience training I felt as if I was trained just the way she wanted.

Eddie wasn't only the nicest man I had ever met; he was also the smartest and he realized, finally, that dogs had distinct personalities. He received a whole new worldview when he saw Cher and I interact. She was a calculating she who seemed to plot ways to get back to me.

Eddie was stunned whenever he saw her benevolence with him turn vindictive with me. But he was also too nice to her. My walks with Cher were almost like sprints because we needed to lose the pounds.

But when Eddie walked her, she stopped to smell the roses, the discards, and sometimes other dogs' poop. A walk with Cher would take Eddie a long time. And any command he delivered was absorbed by those magnificent ears and discarded like ... well, like poop.

After giving Eddie some brief instructions, Cher's nonsense stopped. She visually assassinated me several times as we walked together. Let's face it, I was saving myself. A difficult walk meant that eventually I wouldn't be able to share that fun with him.

Eddie understood that Cher spoke with her eyes. Glares, cuts, and eye-rolls—maybe not exactly the way humans do them, but *moi* recognized them—was part of a language that I had also picked up from the job. Human or canine, those non-verbal cues meant the same things, *Kiss my patootie.*

Cher's understanding of vocabulary had grown. For instance, she understood, "you," "no," "walk," "eat." So if I said, "You no eat" or "no walk you," I wasn't going to be herded, or bullied because the diva had made a decision.

The only times Cher made me feel uncomfortable were during my romantic moments with Eddie. While snuggling, I would catch those huge brown eyes cutting me to ribbons. She wasn't living vicariously through me. I was in the way. Thank God, she was never allowed on our bed. What a curious *ménage à trois* that would be ... yech. At least she understood these words too, "Get out!"

Chapter 5:
Doing Dog Time

Cher and I are survivors. Our relationship has evolved. We discovered that we are stronger together. We have a quiet rhythm.

When my heart was in chaos, she seemed to sense this and offered me her unconditional love. When he, Eddie, the man that we both loved, was around it was only then that Cher's love for me had conditions, opt-out clauses, and terms of agreements.

I didn't mind.

If it hadn't been for Cher, I wouldn't have made it through the tumultuous period in my career. It was a career again and not a job.

I was indebted to Cher for those fat evenings where I moped and ate, and where she just ate, because whenever she placed her head in my lap and allowed me to stroke her, it eased the turmoil in my heart.

I lost the battle with the narcissistic Ms. Right-Hand. Just as it happened in my Master's degree program, I was shoved. At least I wasn't fired, and the place I was shoved to was a better position. So, in essence, I lost but I also won. As mom always said, God can see around corners.

If Ms. Right-Hand hadn't made my work-life such a nightmare, then I wouldn't have felt compelled to do what I never wanted to do, which was to go back to school. If I hadn't gone back to school, I wouldn't have met Eddie. *God can see around corners.*

After Cher and I had married Eddie, we moved into his much larger domicile, a beautiful duplex in an historic neighborhood. I was happily married, and Cher loved the extra room although the privacy fencing kept her from threatening that leap to freedom.

I still gave her morning treats. What else could I do? I had been successfully trained.

My new position was in one of those offices that promoted teleworking to slash office costs. Teleworking has its drawbacks. For one, my remote office is only down the stairs, down the hall, and around the corner from the refrigerator.

As far as the weight thing goes, I'm actually doing better. Eddie is a younger man, and I felt it was a good idea to keep myself attractive. I'm a serious walker, and I was coaxed into yoga by my doctor. The weight started to fall off my thighs and stomach. Hallelujah!

Cher was middle-aged. She suffered from the middle-aged woman's dilemma, an inability to lose weight. No matter how fast or how often we walked, Cher wasn't able to shed her pounds. Plus, she was greedy. She really ought to patent that "I'm starving" look. Or at least present it to moviegoers—she would win an Oscar.

We walked together regularly. Eddie would only help when asked. But too often her only source of exercise was chasing the squirrels in the backyard.

One afternoon I was working from home. It had been a busy day of conference calls and deadlines. I had let Cher out to chase squirrels and, to show her usual disdain for me, by leaving a pile of poo for me to clean up. She was ingenious on where she hid her piles. Summers were the worse, but that's another issue.

I had finally earned my lunch break, and as I approached the back door, I called out to Cher. No response. Then I remembered that I had let her out hours earlier. Suddenly, I had a bad feeling. I ran outside.

No Cher.

I called out to her again in case she was hiding in her usual spots near the shed, behind the tree, under the deck.

No Cher.

Perhaps she was inside, after all. I ran inside the house, calling and checking from room to room. No Cher. I ran back outside and saw evidence that she hadn't vaporized. The beast had dug under the privacy fence and escaped.

At that moment, I remembered that I had taken off her identification tags a few days earlier. The information on the tag was old. It had my premarital name and address. I had taken it off to remind myself to get a newer one made.

Stupid me. I was as rigid as a tree while a quiet panic rose up in my chest. I remembered too many evenings wondering if Cher's old family ever missed her, or if they looked for her still. I remembered wishing there was some way that I could contact them just to let them know that she was safe and content—and fat—and that they didn't need to worry.

"Cher?"

Was living with me really so horrible that she felt compelled to run off?

I took to the streets, running and calling out her name like a crazy woman. I asked strangers if they had seen a fat brown dog with ears like a German shepherd dog and a smirk on her muzzle. No one had seen her. A few offered me sympathy, especially the folks who were walking their dogs.

Cher had disappeared without leaving any clues. I didn't know which direction to head, East or West? I had to admit that she could've absconded hours earlier. Her trail was Siberian cold.

What if she was hurt?

What if some psycho was torturing her?

Eddie was out of town on business. I called him. He wasn't able to offer any words to calm me down. I called Zane. My daughter heard the desperation in my voice and dropped what she was doing to drive through the neighborhood just to catch a glimpse of the wayward pooch.

I got a call late in the evening from the dog pound. *Why didn't I think to call them first? Panic, maybe?* They had discovered Cher's implanted chip under her skin and were able to track me down. She had been found!

I was relieved.

I was going to kill her!

Ironically the dog pound was her destination when I rescued her the first time. It seemed that she found her way there after all.

I was very appreciative when I entered the building. It was strikingly modern, ultra clean, and the staff was very friendly. There was a fee, naturally, and that was when I realized that I had arrived with only lint in my wallet. But no fear, my bank was the next block over.

First, I had to identify my wayward dog. I was taken through double doors to the back rooms where rows of cages held yelping canines. This area looked clean too, but the odor was so strong that it was three-dimensional. I could hardly breathe.

One of the uniformed dog professionals took me to my chip wearer who was on the top tier and she, the usually mute one, was barking her fool head off. It as if she were saying, *get me out of here!* The other dogs almost drowned out her protests by offering to go home with me and live Cher's life of lazy comfort.

It was clearly a contest. Every cage was occupied.

I wished I could take them all home and save their lives.

This time it was my turn to glare, cut, and roll my eyes, although I had to cover my nose and mouth just so that I could breathe. I scanned the card on her cage. I saw where the staff estimated her age as two years old. That was bizarre. Dr. Gorgeous' office had estimated her as being about a year old when I rescued her that first time, six years earlier. How old was Cher really?

I gave her a squint that would've made Samuel L. Jackson envious. "Yeah," I said, "that's her." Then I turned and walked away. She started yapping it up, convinced that I was abandoning her. When I returned from the bank and paid her ransom, I begrudgingly collected the ex-con.

Oh, and she stank too.

I thought I saw relief on her face as she climbed into the car. I slid into the driver's seat and adjusted my rearview mirror. We looked at each other in the mirror, and although she didn't make a sound, I imagined her thoughts. *Thanks, Joy. Did you know they kill bitches up in there? Don't worry. This ain't gonna change a thing between us.*

I did say, "Nice try, diva. You owe me."

Cher and I were survivors. Together we're strong.

Chapter 6:
The Trick with the Babies

I was never ashamed of my plus-sized physique. The media implied that I should've felt shame, but I never did. My husband who was partial, accused me of being beautiful. But I had health issues, and love for myself and my family were my primary reasons to continue to exist.

I tried some things to help me reduce my weight. I walked more, and joined a yoga class. I didn't have the flexibility of a rubber band, so I found the poses kind of humiliating. Especially so when parts of my body wouldn't cooperate as I thought they should.

Dieting? Well, that was a different story. I knew how to fail at dieting. Food had always been my go-to for immediate comfort. In my mind, Heaven was chocolate cake drizzled with chocolate icing.

Sad? My remedy was chocolate.

Happy? Be happier, have some chocolate.

Distressed? Well, why not have chocolate cake with chocolate ice cream.

For my benefit, Eddie did all the cooking. I was forced to eat healthier meals. Dinner meant there was something green on my plate. And who knew that I would love Brussels sprouts? After all, the name of the vegetable sounded kind of disgusting. Brussels was sprouting? But what was it sprouting?

What did my health have to do with Cher? Everything, because she was trying to kill me. Follow my logic and then judge.

Chapter 6: The Trick with the Babies

I take medications. My family history dictated that I wouldn't live long past fifty. My siblings and I, based on both the maternal and paternal sides of our family, were likely to keel over from a stroke or heart attack. Diabetes didn't run in my family; it sprinted. I was diagnosed with high blood pressure, which was reason enough for Eddie to cut out salt and fried food from my meals.

A side effect of my high blood pressure medication caused me to relieve my bladder in the wee—pun intended—hours of the night. Having to urinate in the middle of the night is quite disruptive to a good night's sleep. For me, the need would happen suddenly. One minute I'd be having the loveliest dream, perhaps dancing with Idris Elba in Paris under a canopy of stars, and the next minute I'd be wide awake and scudding across the room to empty a bladder that had been drained before bedtime.

These interruptions didn't often happen, but they did occur enough times to make me sleep deficient by the end of the week. Like everything else, it had gotten worse with age.

My trusty pooch could be counted on to see an opportunity in something as troublesome as a late night relieve.

Whenever I'd awaken in the predawn morning, I tended to be a little disoriented. I had learned—or was trained—that running full speed to the bathroom, in the dark, can be risky. On purpose.

Why?

She wanted to get rid of me. She wanted Eddie all to herself.

That was all I can think of when I would trip on her baby. The toy usually squeaked out in protest after my foot deflated its plastic body. Most of the time, I won't go down. I would just get plain annoyed because I knew that she took the time to plot my path and place her toy in the most inconvenient place … for me. Her ultimate goal, I was certain, was for me to trip, fall, and break my neck.

Sometimes she won. There have been times during the darkest night, when my eyes were heavily stitched together with sleep that I would trip on the abused toy, and go down on knees that were quickly losing cartilage. Two things kept me from screaming at her. One, I didn't want to wake Eddie. Two, I didn't want to feed her the excitement of near victory.

Keep in mind her baby was never in the bedroom before bedtime. It was only dropped in place after I went to sleep.

Cher's diabolical.

She was also resourceful and has used her babies in other similar circumstances. Oh yes, her babies get moved around the house. It used to be cute seeing Cher toting one of them from room to room in that maternal trot as she carried a baby in her mouth. What wasn't cute was when she *accidently* left a baby in less than conspicuous places.

She has made me suspicious.

Our home had one set of stairs that led up to the office and bedrooms. Cher's favorite room was of course Eddie's appointed "man cave."

Chapter 6: The Trick with the Babies

Whenever she and I were alone in the home, she was apt to go into his cave, with a baby and stay there until he arrived. Other times, she lingered in his room, alone.

Where was the baby?

Cher and I were both predictable creatures. For instance, we take the stairs the same way. Her preference was the left side of the stairs while I always traveled on the right side. The hallway was poorly lit, and she also knew which side of the stairs I tended to run. If she was running up and down on the left side, then why was her baby dropped on the right. In fact, I will go further and state that she deliberately placed her baby in the darkest part of the step so that I couldn't see it.

The baby was never there when I go up the stairs. Thank God for banisters. The opportunistic mongrel wasn't quite as smart as she had hoped.

Chapter 7:
Take What You Want Just Let Me Outta Here

I know that I haven't mentioned Mario for several chapters. I also know this tale is about Cher, but I have to point out again the differences between the dogs.

Zane and I had lived harmoniously for years in a suburban neighborhood without the benefit of electronic alarms. We had Mario. No one made it onto our driveway without his barking. No one entered the house without a ruthless inspection. To put it bluntly, if someone didn't live in the house, then they didn't pass Mario's test. His true Dalmatian smile was a snarl, and it wasn't pretty.

Cher loved everybody. She was often offended when I pulled her back from greeting strangers. She would approach them with her ears lowered, as if expecting a head rub, and when she wagged her tail, her whole body got in the motion.

There was a time when I had called a local pet store to set up a bathing appointment for Cher. When questioned about her breed, I naively stated that she was a dingo. Suddenly I was laughed at ... laughed at? I was also told that I couldn't bring in my feral beast for grooming.

Really? A feral beast?

I wasn't talking about the groomer's mother, I was asking for a service for my friendly pooch. Was that too much? Did that statement sound like Cher?

My point is that dingoes, like pit bulls, are labeled. All dogs have distinct personalities. Sometimes the answer is nurture and not nature. Again, my dingo was friendly, and my Dalmatian was ... well, ferocious.

There are times when ferocious is necessary.

I was an early riser, but not on purpose. Or should I have said, not naturally. Our alarms sounded at four in the morning. I was usually at work by six.

The good points of being up insanely early were that, when not teleworking, I was in the office and there was no one else there to meddle or mingle. Not only could I get things done before the crew came in, I also got to leave early too.

The bad point? It was four in the morning.

Sometimes Eddie had to peel my fingers off the pillow and guide me to the bathroom. Usually I was a babbling, drooling idiot grabbing hold of the bathroom sink for support. Only after my first cup of chocolate flavored coffee did I become more human and less zombie.

One chilly morning, I remember scampering for the car. I also remember anticipating the frigid jolt of reality on my buttocks from the car's leather seat. I saw by his manner that Eddie was concerned about something other than a cold tush.

He poked me and nodded at the men on the corner. They were huddled together under a streetlamp. I couldn't see their faces, but I didn't think it odd. He went back inside the house and did a strange thing. He set the alarm. Eddie was a former combat soldier who continued to serve as a reservist. I trusted his instincts. Besides, the only danger I ever faced was a challenge of road rage on the interstate.

Later as I was pouring over a spreadsheet, my personal cell phone rang. The caller was a teacher from the elementary school two blocks from our house. She had gotten my number from Cher's new identification tag.

Moments later my desk phone rang. Eddie had spoken with the police. Our security alarm had sounded. He was leaving his office to meet the police.

I told him about the teacher's call and said, "Be careful, Cher couldn't open the door. Dogs don't have thumbs."

I arrived home to see that we'd been hit. The alarm had prevented a thorough robbery, so the thieves had opted for a crash and grab. Eddie surveyed the damage as detectives poured over possible clues. I was heartbroken, and I felt trampled on.

We estimated that they had kicked in the back door. Our privacy fence had probably shielded their actions. Thank God Eddie saw what I had missed. I had worn my not-in-my-respectable-neighborhood shroud. Was I wrong not to nurse a healthy skepticism about a group of men standing idly on a corner in the early morning hours? Although I hadn't served my country in a conflict half a world away, I still should've been cautious.

What about Cher?

Our home had been ransacked. Items had been stolen or simply tossed. Luckily those turds hadn't enough time to take the big items. We had all our electronics. We were lucky.

Cher was lucky.

She had been no threat to them. The fierce dingo, the feral beast, had managed to puddle near a window. An open door led to her escape where she ran up to some schoolchildren who probably soothed her frayed nerves.

All I usually got from her was an attitude!

Maybe her demeanor saved her life? I've contemplated that sometimes. I've often imagined how that scenario would've played out if Mario had been at the house instead. He could've behaved like other dogs by barking his head off and thwarted the intrusion, but more likely, he would've remained silent until the first one entered the house and then ... well, a fleshy thigh, also known as breakfast, would've been served.

In a confrontation, Mario could've been harmed or worse. Of the two, Cher was always the smarter dog.

Chapter 8:
A-Muse Thing

I had delusions of being a writer, but not just any writer, a successful writer. Before personal computers, before tablets, and cell phones there were books. I loved television and had my favorite shows, but it was books that saved me from boredom. I picked up a pen first and then took typing classes when they weren't cool. I wanted to be just like Toni Morrison or Stephen King or Anne Rice. There was no harm in having such a high goal. Achieving it? Well, that was something else.

I wanted to scare the crap out of people, but in a good way. Real horror stories exist all around us. Just open up a newspaper or tap a news icon on your tablet or computer. Scary stuff!

I wrote several novels that didn't pass editorial muster. I thought they were good, but I took the hint. I stopped writing.

I decided to revisit my writing while I was in the MBA marketing class. My professor was a douche who gave social media the short shrift, but he did tell the tale of a South American fashion house that had challenged the established protocols. The fashion house hadn't been part of the traditional culture with a stable of highbrow fashion designers anchored in New York, London, or Paris. Despite bucking the norm, it became profitable. At the same time, I discovered that Amazon was offering wannabes like me a shot at literary immortality.

On a walk with Cher, a noticeably humbler Miss Cher since her incarceration, I considered this option. I had an old story about a vampire … yes, another hunky vampire love story. It was worthy of another look-see.

That was how it started.

I dusted off the old manuscript and either tweaked or rewrote entire chapters. When the twisty plot didn't suspend disbelief, I walked Cher. Somehow our easy cadences and the music in my headphones inspired me to make my gritty, and graphic vampire tale more gothic. Truthfully, I have no hope of being successful as a writer. That's okay.

*   *   *

My life is filling out. I do voluntary work helping children. It is my way of leaving the world a little bit better than I found it.

My relationship with Zane has improved to the point where I can see us as being close again. After all, now that she is a parent too, she realizes that I wasn't the enemy overdosing on stupidity.

I'm enjoying my love affair with Eddie, and my career is on track.

But, life is not all chocolate cake—cue the scary music.

She watches me still, probably plotting my demise. She loves and hates me with the same intensity. What would I do without her? What would I do without my Cher?

The End.

Thank You

I hope you will leave a review.

Sign up for my mailing list and get a FREE copy of my book of short stories, Fantasies in the DayMare Zone, plus a bonus copy of my Award Winning Paranormal/Supernatural novel, Cesar, The Demon Lover's Chronicles: https://www.subscribepage.com/x0c5t1

About the Author:

Julian Coleman is a Southern author who enjoys reading, writing, and running.

Please be on the lookout for her upcoming books. Join me:

Website: http://www.JulianColeman.net

Email: JulianMColeman@gmail.com

Facebook: https://www.facebook.com/JulianMColeman

Twitter: https://twitter.com/JulianMColeman1

www.ingramcontent.com/pod-product-compliance
Lightning Source LLC
Chambersburg PA
CBHW071218130626
46555CB00004B/1751